P9-DNM-716

A COUNTRY FAR AWAY

A COUNTRY FAR AWAY

Story by
NIGEL GRAY

Pictures by
PHILIPPE DUPASQUIER

ORCHARD BOOKS · NEW YORK

Text copyright © 1988 by Nigel Gray
Illustrations copyright © 1988 by Philippe Dupasquier
First published in Great Britain by Andersen Press Ltd.
First American hardcover edition 1989 published by Orchard Books
First Orchard Paperbacks edition 1991

All rights reserved. No part of this book may be reproduced or transmitted
in any form or by any means, electronic or mechanical, including
photocopying, recording or by any information storage or retrieval system,
without permission in writing from the Publisher.

Orchard Books
95 Madison Avenue, New York, NY 10016
Manufactured in the United States of America
Book design by Mina Greenstein
The text of this book is set in 20 pt. Garamond No. 3.
Hardcover   6   8   10   9   7
Paperback   6   8   10   9

Library of Congress Cataloging-in-Publication Data
Gray, Nigel. A country far away / story by Nigel Gray; pictures by
Philippe Dupasquier. — 1st American ed.   p.   cm.
Summary: Side-by-side pictures reveal the essential similarities between the
lives of two boys, one in a western country, one in a rural African village.
ISBN 0-531-05792-5 (tr.)   ISBN 0-531-08392-6 (lib. bdg.)
ISBN 0-531-07024-7 (pbk.)
[1. Manners and customs—Fiction.]   I. Dupasquier, Philippe, ill.
II. Title.   PZ7.G7813Co   1989   88-22360   CIP   AC

A COUNTRY FAR AWAY

Today was an ordinary day. I stayed home.

I helped my mom and dad.

They were pleased.

Today was the last day of school before vacation.

We went home early.

I went bike riding with my friends. I'm one of the best riders.

My mom had a baby. We can't decide what to call her.

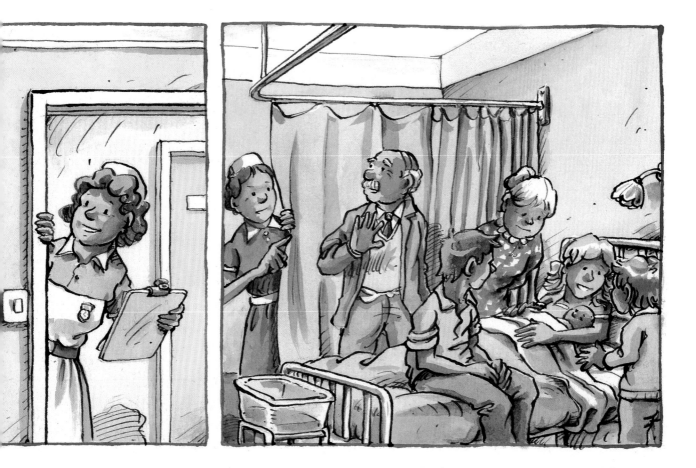

Today it rained—so we went swimming.

Today we went into town to do some shopping.

I thought we were never going to get there.

We had to get many things. It was fun.

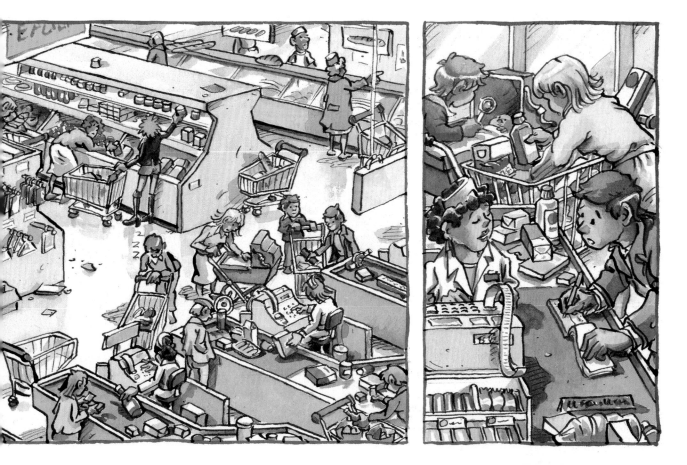

Then we had a celebration for my baby sister.

We had our photograph taken.

Today we played soccer. I scored a goal.

My cousin came to visit. We stayed up late.

Today I looked at some pictures of a country far away.

I'd like to go there someday…

…and make a friend.